Disney
Tigger's Treasure

Written by
Guy Davis

Illustrated by
Dean Kleven

© Disney Enterprises, Inc.
Based on the "Winnie the Pooh" works, by A.A. Milne and E.H. Shepard.
All Rights Reserved.

Published by
Louis Weber, C.E.O.
Publications International, Ltd.
7373 North Cicero Avenue
Lincolnwood, Illinois 60712

www.pilbooks.com

Manufactured in China.

8 7 6 5 4 3 2 1

ISBN 1-4127-3023-6

It was a great day for playing outside. In fact, it was an absolutely perfect day to play outside.

"Not too hot, not too cold. A perfect playing day!" said Pooh to his friends Tigger and Piglet.

"But...what shall we play?" asked Piglet. The friends thought and thought.

"Ahoy there, mates!" said Tigger playfully. "I have an idea that will shiver your timbers!"

After Tigger explained his idea, the friends gathered a few things. They climbed into a big old tree and pretended they were on a boat.

"Captain Tigger," said Pooh, "we're ready to set sail!"

The three friends imagined that they were sailing the seven seas. They felt the warm ocean breeze on their faces.

They saw great blue whales and friendly dolphins, too.
Suddenly, Captain Tigger cried out, "Land ho!"

"Er, what should we do now?" asked Piglet as they climbed up on shore.

"We should do what tiggers do best," he said. "We should look for buried treasure!"

"Do we have a map?" asked Pooh.

"We don't need a map!" Tigger answered. "We just need to find an X, 'cause X marks the spot!"

So the three adventurers began searching for treasure!

They looked high. They looked low. They looked near, and they looked far. In fact, they looked all around the Hundred-Acre Wood! But no matter where they looked, they didn't see any Xs marking any spots.

A bit tired, the friends sat down to rest a little.

"Think, think, think," pondered Pooh. "Where haven't we looked?"

Piglet piped up, "Christopher Robin always says not to forget to look under your nose!"

Tigger looked under his nose... and looked at the crisscrossed logs they had been sitting on.

"Hoo-hoo-hoo!" hollered Tigger.
"We found it! X marks the spot!"
Taking turns with the shovel, the
friends began to dig, and dig, and dig.
"There's no treasure here,"
announced Tigger, "just bugs! Blech!"

The three friends sat down next to the big hole they had dug. They were disappointed that there wasn't any treasure there.

"X marks the spot," said Tigger. "Harumph! There's nothing here in this spot but us."

Piglet jumped up. "Maybe that's it!" he said. "Maybe *we're* it!"

"There is a treasure here at the X,"
continued Piglet. "It's us!"
    The three adventurers looked at
each other and smiled.

"Aye aye, Piglet," said Captain Tigger. "I think you're right! We did find a treasure, and it was right under our noses!"

The three best buddies had discovered a treasure after all... a treasure called friendship.